THE HISTORY

OF

SIR RICHARD WHITTINGTON.

BY T. H.

EDITED, WITH AN INTRODUCTON,

BY

HENRY B. WHEATLEY, F.S.A.

LONDON:

PRINTED FOR THE VILLON SOCIETY.

1885.

Introduction.

THE popular story of Whittington and his Cat is one in which a version of a wide-spread folk-tale has been grafted upon the history of the life of an historical character, and in the later versions the historical incidents have been more and more eliminated. The three chief points in the chap-book story are, 1, the poor parentage of the hero; 2, his change of mind at Highgate Hill by reason of hearing Bow Bells; and, 3, his good fortune arising from the sale of his cat. Now these are all equally untrue as referring to the historical Whittington, and the second is apparently an invention of the eighteenth century. When the Rev. Canon Lysons wrote his interesting and valuable work entitled *The Model Merchant* he showed the incorrectness of the first point by tracing out Whittington's distinguished pedigree, but he was loath to dispute the other two. It is rather strange that neither Mr. Lysons nor Messrs. Besant and Rice appear to have seen the work which I now present to my readers, which is the earliest form of the life of Whittington known to exist. This is

printed from the copy in the Pepysian Library, a later edition
of which, with a few typographical alterations, will be found in
the British Museum library. This *History* will be found to
differ very considerably from the later and better-known story,
which appears to have been written early in the eighteenth
century. A comparison between the latter which I print at
the end of this Preface (p. xxix.) with T. H.'s earlier text will
not, I think, be found unprofitable. *The Famous and Remarkable
History* here reprinted is undated, but was probably published
about 1670; the later edition in the British Museum is dated
1678. One passage on page 7—" The merchant went then to
the Exchange, which was then in Lumber-street, about his
affairs"—seems to show that it was originally written quite
early in the century, and it is just possible that T. H. stands for
the voluminous playwright and pamphleteer Thomas Heywood.
The Exchange was removed to its present site in 1568, and
therefore our tract could not have been written before that date,
but must have appeared when the memory of the old meeting-
place was still fresh in public memory. On page 11 it will be
seen that Whittington, when discontented with his position in
Fitzwarren's house, set out before day-break on All Hallows-
day with his clothes in a bundle, in order to seek his fortune
elsewhere. He had only got as far as Bunhill when he heard
Bow bells ring out what appeared to be—

"Turn again, Whittington, Lord Mayor of London,
Turn again, Whittington, Lord Mayor of London."

These words took complete possession of him, and he returned before it was known that he had run away. In the more modern chap-book Whittington is made to reach Holloway, where it would be less easy to hear Bow bells, and from which place he would have found it more difficult to return before the cook had risen. As far as I can find there is no allusion to Holloway or Highgate hill in any early version, and it is evident that this localization is quite modern. Mr. Lysons is certainly wrong when he says that at Highgate " a stone continued to mark the spot for many centuries." It is not known when the stone was first erected there, but it was probably put up when the name of the place was first foisted into the tale. One stone was taken away in 1795, but others have succeeded it, and now there is a Whittington Stone Tavern; and the situation of Whittington College, which was removed to Highgate in 1808, has helped to favour the supposition that Whittington himself was in some way connected with that place.

The form of invitation which the bells rung out varies very much in the different versions.

In Richard Johnson's ballad (1612) we find—

> " Whittington, back return."

which is then amplified into—

> " Turn againe, Whittington,
> For thou in time shall grow
> Lord Maior of London."

In T. H.'s *History* (see p. 11) we have—

"Turn again, Whittington, Lord Mayor of London."

In the later chap-book version this is altered into—

"Turn again, Whittington,
    Lord Mayor of great London."

It will be seen that the special reference to the fact that Whittington was three times Lord Mayor is not to be found in either the ballads or the chap-books.

In the *Life*, by the author of *George Barnwell* (1811), however we read—

"Return again, Whittington,
    Thrise Lord Mayor of London."

And in *The Life and Times of Whittington* (1841)—

"Turn again, turn again, Whittington,
    Three times Lord Mayor of London."

In the early version of the *History* by T. H. the fanciful portions are only allowed to occupy a small portion of the whole, and a long account is given of Whittington's real actions, but, in the later chap-book versions, the historical incidents are ruthlessly cut down, and the fictitious ones amplified. This will be seen by comparing the two printed here. Thus T. H. merely says (p. 6) that Whittington was obscurely born, and that being almost starved in the country he came up to London. In the later chap-book the journey to London is more fully enlarged upon (p. xxxiii.), and among those at Whittington's marriage with Alice Fitzwarren the name of the Company of Stationers not then in existence is foisted in (pp. xlii.) It does not appear in T. H.'s *History.*

In many other particulars the later chap-book which contains the story as known to modern readers is amplified, and thus shows signs of a very late origin.

With regard to the three fictitious points of Whittington's history mentioned at the beginning of this preface, the first—his poor parentage—is disposed of by documentary evidence; the second—his sitting on a stone at Highgate hill—has been shown to be quite a modern invention; and the third—the story of the cat—has been told of so many other persons in different parts of the world that there is every reason to believe it to be a veritable folk-tale joined to the history of Whittington from some unexplained connection. None of the early historians who mention Whittington allude to the incident of the cat, and it is only to be found in popular literature, ballads, plays, &c. The story seems to have taken its rise in the reign of Queen Elizabeth. The reason why however the life of Whittington should have been chosen as the stock upon which this folk-tale should be grafted is still unexplained. Some have supposed that he obtained his money by the employment of "cats," or vessels for the carriage of coals; but this suggestion does not appear to be worthy of much consideration.

It is said that at Newgate, which owed much to Whittington, there was a statue of him with a cat, which was destroyed in the Great Fire; and in 1862, when some alterations were made in an old house at Gloucester, which had been occupied by the Whittington family until 1460, a stone was said to have been dug up on which was a basso-relievo representing he figure of a boy carrying a cat in his arms. This find, however, appears rather suspicious.

Keightley devotes a whole chapter of his *Tales and Popular Fictions* to the legend of Whittington and his Cat, in which he points out how many similar stories exist. The *Facezie,* of Arlotto, printed soon after the author's death in 1483, contain a tale of a merchant of Genoa, entitled "Novella delle Gatte," and probably from this the story came to England, although it is also found in a German chronicle of the thirteenth century. Sir William Ouseley, in his *Travels,* 1819, speaking of an island in the Persian Gulf, relates, on the authority of a Persian MS., that " in the tenth century, one Keis, the son of a poor widow in Siráf, embarked for India with a cat, his only property. There he fortunately arrived at a time when the palace was so infested by mice or rats that they invaded the king's food, and persons were employed to drive them from the royal banquet. Keis produced his cat; the noxious animals soon disappeared, and magnificent rewards were bestowed on the adventurer of Siráf, who returned to that city, and afterwards, with his mother and brothers, settled on the island, which from him has been denominated Keis, or according to the Persians Keisch." Mr. Halliwell-Phillipps quotes from the *Description of Guinea* (1665) the record of " how Alphonso, a Portuguese, being wrecked on the coast of Guinney, and being presented by the king thereof with his weight in gold for a cat to kill their mice; and an oyntment to kill their flies, which he improved within five years to 6000*l.* in the place, and, returning to Portugal after fifteen years traffick, became the third man in the kingdom." *

Keightley also quotes two similar stories from Thiele's *Danish Popular Traditions* and another from the letters of Count Magalotti, a Florentine of the latter half of the seventeenth century.

Mr. Lysons gives much information as to the great value of cats in the Middle Ages, but the writer of the *History of Whittington* does not lead us to believe that they were dear in England, for he makes the boy buy his cat for one penny. The two following titles are from the Stationers' Registers. The ballad is probably the one subsequently referred to as by Richard Johnson:—

" The History of Richard Whittington, of his lowe birthe, his great fortune, as yt was plaied by the Prynces Servants. Licensed to Thomas Pavyer, Feb. 8, 1604-5."

" A Ballad, called The vertuous lyfe and memorable death of Sir Richard Whittington, mercer, sometymes Lord Maiour

* *Catalogue of Chap Books, Garlands, &c.* 1849, p. 69.

of the honorable Citie of London. Licensed to John Wright, 16 July, 1605."

The first reference that we find to the cat incident is in the play *Eastward Hoe* by Chapman, Ben Jonson, and Marston; for, as the portrait which was said to have existed at Mercers' Hall is not now known, it can scarcely be put in evidence. This half-length portrait of a man of about sixty years of age, dressed in a livery gown and black cap of the time of Henry VIII. with a figure of a black and white cat on the left, is said to have had painted in the left-hand upper corner of the canvas the inscription, " R. Whittington, 1536."

In *Eastward Hoe*, 1605, Touchstone assures Goulding that he hopes to see him reckoned one of the worthies of the city of London "When the famous fable of Whittington and his puss shall be forgotten."

The next allusion is in Thomas Heywood's *If you know not me, you know nobody*, 2nd part, 1606.

Dean Nowell. " This Sir Richard Whittington, three times Mayor,
　　Sonne to a knight and prentice to a mercer,
　　Began the Library of Grey-Friars in London,
　　And his executors after him did build
　　Whittington Colledge, thirteene Alms-houses for poore men,
　　Repair'd S. Bartholomewes, in Smithfield,
　　Glased the Guildhall, and built Newgate.
Hobson. Bones of men, then I have heard lies ;
　　For I have heard he was a scullion,
　　And rais'd himself by venture of a cat.
Nowell. They did the more wrong to the gentleman."

Here it will be seen that, although the popular tale is mentioned, it is treated as a mere invention unworthy of credence.

The next in point of time is the ballad by Richard Johnson, published in the *Crowne Garland of Goulden Roses* (1612), which probably had a much earlier existence in a separate form. It is the earliest form of the story of Whittington now in existence.

A song of Sir Richard Whittington, who by strange fortunes came to bee thrice Lord Maior of London; with his bountifull guifts and liberallity given to this honourable Citty.

(To the tune of " *Dainty come thou to me.*")

"Here must I tell the praise
    Of worthie Whittington,
Known to be in his dayes
    Thrice Maior of London.
But of poor parentage
    Borne was he, as we heare,
And in his tender age
    Bred up in Lancashire.

Poorely to London than
    Came up this simple lad,
Where, with a marchant-man,
    Soone he a dwelling had ;
And in a kitchen plast,
    A scullion for to be,
Whereas long time he past
    In labour grudgingly.

His daily service was
   Turning spits at the fire ;
And to scour pots of brasse,
   For a poore scullions hire.
Meat and drinke all his pay,
   Of coyne he had no store ;
Therefore to run away,
   In secret thought he bore.

So from this marchant-man
   Whittington secretly
Towards his country ran,
   To purchase liberty.
But as he went along
   In a fair summer's morne,
London bells sweetly rung,
   'Whittington, back return !'

'Evermore sounding so,
   Turn againe, Whittington ;
For thou in time shall grow
   Lord-Maior of London.'
Whereupon back againe
   Whittington came with speed,
Aprentise to remaine,
   As the Lord had decreed.

'Still blessed be the bells'
   (This was his daily song),
'They my good fortune tells,
   Most sweetly have they rung.

If God so favour me,
  I will not proove unkind ;
London my love shall see,
  And my great bounties find.'

But see his happy chance !
  This scullion had a cat,
Which did his state advance,
  And by it wealth he gat.
His maister ventred forth,
  To a land far unknowne,
With marchandize of worth,
  And is in stories shewne.

Whittington had no more
  But this poor cat as than,
Which to the ship he bore,
  Like a brave marchant-man.
' Vent'ring the same,' quoth he,
  ' I may get store of golde,
And Maior of London be,
  As the bells have me told.'

Whittington's marchandise,
  Carried was to a land
Troubled with rats and mice,
  As they did understand.
The king of that country there,
  As he at dinner sat,
Daily remain'd in fear
  Of many a mouse and rat.

Introduction.

Meat that in trenchers lay,
  No way they could keepe safe ;
But by rats borne away,
  Fearing no wand or staff.
Whereupon, soone they brought
  Whittington's nimble cat ;
Which by the king was bought ;
  Heapes of gold giv'n for that.

Home againe came these men
  With their ships loaden so ;
Whittington's wealth began
  By this cat thus to grow.
Scullions life he forsooke
  To be a marchant good,
And soon began to looke
  How well his credit stood.

After that he was chose
  Shriefe of the citty heere,
And then full quickly rose
  Higher as did appeare.
For to this cities praise
  Sir Richard Whittington
Came to be in his dayes
  Thrise Maior of London.

More his fame to advance,
  Thousands he lent his king
To maintaine warres in France,
  Glory from thence to bring.

And after, at a feast,
  Which he the king did make,
He burnt the bonds all in jeast,
  And would no money take.

Ten thousand pound he gave
  To his prince willingly,
And would not one penny have.
  This in kind courtesie.
God did thus make him great,
  So would he daily see
Poor people fed with meat,
  To shew his charity.

Prisoners poore cherish'd were,
  Widdowes sweet comfort found ;
Good deeds, both far and neere,
  Of him do still resound.
Whittington Colledge is
  One of his charities,
Records reporteth this
  To lasting memories.

Newgate he builded faire,
  For prisoners to live in ; .
Christ's Church he did repaire,
  Christian love for to win.
Many more such like deedes
  Were done by Whittington ;
Which joy and comfort breedes,
  To such as looke thereon.

c

> Lancashire thou hast bred
>   This flower of charity;
> Though he be gone and dead,
>   Yet lives he lastingly.
> Those bells that call'd him so,
>   'Turne again, Whittington,'
> Call you back may moe
>   To live so in London."

This ballad, as it stands here with the exception of the last stanza, was reprinted in *A Collection of Old Ballads*, 1823, vol. i. p. 130.

This ballad is the original of all the later ballads, although the titles have been greatly varied. The Roxburghe ballad (vol. iii. p. 58) is dated in the British Museum Catalogue 1641 [?]. Its full title is as follows :—

"London's Glory and Whittington's Renown, or a Looking Glass for Citizens of London, being a remarkable story how Sir Richard Whittington (a poor boy bred up in Lancashire) came to be three times Lord Mayor of London in three several kings' reigns, and how his rise was by a cat, which he sent by a venture beyond sea. Together with his bountiful gifts and liberality given to this honourable City, and the vast sums of money he lent the King to maintain the wars in France; and how at a great Feast, to which he invited the King, the Queen, and the Nobility, he generously burnt the writings and freely forgave his Majesty the whole Debt. Tune of 'Dainty, come

thou to me.' London : Printed for R. Burton, at the Horse
Shoe in West Smithfield."

The bulk of the ballad is the same as Richard Johnson's,
but the following first stanza is added, the original first stanza
becoming the second :—

> " Brave London Prentices,
>   Come listen to my song,
> Tis for your glory all
>   And to you both belong.
> And you poor country lads,
>   Though born of low degree,
> See by God's providence
>   What you in time may be."

The second half of the original seventh stanza, and the eighth,
ninth, and tenth stanzas, are left out.

Immediately before the last stanza the following one is
introduced :—

> " Let all kynde Citizens
>   Who do this story read,
> By his example learn
>   Always the poor to feed.
> What is lent to the poor
>   The Lord will sure repay,
> And blessings keep in store
>   Until the latter day."

The other alterations are not many, and chiefly consist in
transpositions by which the rhymes are varied. This may be

seen by comparing with the original the Roxburghe version of
the last stanza which is as follows :—

> " Lancashire, thou hast bred
>   This flower of charity ;
>   Though he be dead and gone,
>   Yet lives his memory.
>   Those bells that call'd him so,
>   Turn again, Whittington,
>   Would they call may moe
>   Such men to fair London."

At the end of one of the chap-books there is a version of the
ballad in which Lancashire is replaced by Somersetshire.

In the same volume of the *Roxburghe Ballads* (p. 470) is a
short version [1710?] containing a few only of the verses taken
from the ballad. It is illustrated with some woodcuts from
T. H.'s earlier *History*.

" An old Ballad of Whittington and his Cat, who from a poor
boy came to be thrice Lord Mayor of London. Printed and
sold in Aldermary Church Yard, London."

There is a copy of this in the Chetham Library.

The following are some of the chief references to Whittington's
story in literature after the publication of Johnson's ballad,
arranged in chronological order : —

> " As if a new-found Whittington's rare cat,
>   Come to extoll their birth-rights above that
>   Which nature once intended."—
>
> Stephens's *Essayes and Characters*, 1615.

" Faith, how many churches do you mean to build
  Before you die ?   Six bells in every steeple,
  And let them all go to the *City tune,*
  Turn again, Whittington, and who they say
  Grew rich, and let his land out for nine lives,
  'Cause all came in by a cat."——

         Shirley's *Constant Maid* (1640), act ii. sc. 2.

"I have heard of Whittington and his cat, and others, that have made fortunes by strange means."—Parson's *Wedding* (1664).

Pepys went on September 21, 1668, to Southwark Fair, "and there saw the puppet show of Whittington, which was pretty to see." He adds in his *Diary* "how that idle thing do work upon people that see it, and even myself too."

In the *Tatler* of September 13, 1709 (No. 67), is a list of great men to be entered in the Temple of Fame, and in the subsequent No. 78 is printed the following letter from a Citizen :—

" Mr. Isaac Bickerstaff, Sir, Your *Tatler* of September 13 I am now reading, and in your list of famous men desire you not to forget Alderman Whittington, who began the world with a cat, and died worth three hundred and fifty thousand pounds sterling, which he left to an only daughter three years after his mayoralty. If you want any further particulars of ditto Alderman, daughter, or cat, let me know, and per first will advise the needful, which concludes, Your loving Friend, LEMUEL LEGER."

" I am credibly informed that there was once a design of casting into an opera the story of Whittington and his Cat, and that in order to it there had been got together a great quantity of mice ;

but Mr. Rich, the proprietor of the playhouse, very prudently considered that it would be impossible for the cat to kill them all, and that consequently the princes of the stage might be as much infested with mice as the prince of the island was before the cat's arrival upon it; for which reason he would not permit it to be acted in his house."—*Spectator* (No. 5, March 6, 1711).

The Rev. Samuel Pegge brought the subject of Whittington and his Cat before a meeting of the Society of Antiquaries in 1771, but he could make nothing at all of the cat. There is no record of the inquiry in the *Archaeologia*, but it is mentioned in a letter from Gough to Tyson, 27 Dec. 1771 (Nichols's *Literary Anecdotes*, vol. viii. p. 575). Horace Walpole was annoyed at the Society for criticising his "Richard III." and in his *Short Notes on his Life* he wrote—"Foote having brought them on the stage for sitting in council, as they had done on Whittington and his Cat, I was not sorry to find them so ridiculous, or to mark their being so, and upon that nonsense, and the laughter that accompanied it, I struck my name out of their book."

Foote brought out his comedy of *The Nabob* at the Haymarket Theatre in 1772. Sir Matthew Mite, the hero of the piece, is elected a member of the Society of Antiquaries, and delivers an address on Whittington and his Cat in which he gave the following solution of the difficulty :—"The commerce this worthy merchant carried on was chiefly confined to our coasts. For this purpose he constructed a vessel which for its agility and lightness he aptly christened a cat. Nay, to this our day, gentlemen, all our coals from Newcastle are imported in nothing but cats. From thence it appears that it was not the whiskered four-footed, mouse-killing cat that was the source of the magistrate's wealth, but the coasting, sailing, coal-carrying cat; that, gentlemen, was Whittington's cat."

We may now pass from the fictitious to the real Richard Whittington, and although this is not the place for a life of the distinguished citizen, which may be found elsewhere, it will be convenient to set down in order the chief incidents of his career.

Richard Whittington was the third son of Sir William Whittington, knight, of Pauntley, Gloucestershire, and it is assumed, by some writers, that he was born in or about the year 1360. We must, however, place his birth at an earlier date, for his name appears in the city *Letter Book,* H, fol. 110*a*, (as Richard Whyttingdone), in the second year of Richard II. (A.D. 1379), as a contributor of five marks towards a loan to the city authorities; about four-fifths of the subscribers contributing the same, which is the lowest figure among the contributions.* This is the first appearance of Whittington's name in the city books. William, the eldest son, succeeded to the family property of Pauntley, but, dying without issue, the estate went to Robert, the second son, who became high sheriff of the county in 1402, and again in 1407. Pauntley remained in the family as late as 1546.

* Riley's *Memorials of London and London Life,* p. 534 (note).

Nothing is known of Richard's early life, either as to when or how he came to London. He appears to have married Alice, daughter of Hugh Fitzwarren, and probably he was originally apprenticed to his father-in-law, whose name appears in all the versions of his history.

The second appearance of Whittington's name in the city books is in 8 Richard II., when he was one of the eight common councilmen for Coleman Street ward. In 11 Richard II. he is named as becoming surety to the chamberlain in the sum of ten pounds towards providing money for defence of the city. In the following year he appears to have been no longer a member for Coleman Street ward. On the 12th of March, 1393, he is named as then chosen alderman of Broad Street ward; and on 21st September of the same year he was chosen by the mayor, William Staundon, one of the sheriffs for the ensuing year.*

When Adam Bamme died in the year 1397, during his mayoralty, Richard II. arbitrarily put Whittington in his place, and at the lord mayor's day of that year Whittington again filled the office, being then regularly elected.† From his will we find that this king, who was a member of the Mercers' Company, to which Whittington was apprenticed, was an especial patron of his. In 1400 he was excused from attending the Scottish wars, and in 1406 he was again elected mayor. He

* Riley's *Memorials*, pp. 533-4.
† The Royal Mandate, dated June 8, is printed in Riley's *Memorials*, p. 545.

rebuilt his parish church, and Mr. Riley has printed in his valuable *Memorials* (p. 578) the grant by Whittington of land for the re-building of the church of St. Michael, Paternoster, "in the street called La Riole," called after the merchants of La Riole, a town near Bordeaux, who had established themselves there.

Whittington was knighted by Henry V., and in 1419 he was elected mayor for the fourth time. It was in this year that John Carpenter commenced the compilation of his famous *Liber Albus.* We see how highly this distinguished citizen was appreciated from the writings of such men as Grafton and Stow. Richard Grafton writes in his *Chronicle* (1569, p. 433)—

" This yere (1406) a worthie citizen of London, named Rychard Whittyngton, mercer and alderman, was elected maior of the sayde citie, and bare that office three tymes. This worshipfull man so bestowed his goodes and substaunce to the honor of God, to the reliefe of the pore, and to the benefite of the comon weale, that he hath right well deserved to be regestered in the boke of fame. First, he erected one house or church in London to be a house of prayer, and he named the same after his awne name Whittyngtons College, and so it remayneth to this day. And in the same church, besydes certeine priestes and clerkes, he placed a number of poore aged men and women and buylded for them houses and lodgyngs, and allowed unto them wood, cole, cloth, and weekly money to their great reliefe and comfort. . . . . . He also buylded for the ease of the maior of London and his brethren, and of the worshipfull

d

citizens at the solempne dayes of their assemblye, a chapell adioining to the Guyldhall, to the entent they should euer before they entered into any of theyr affayrs first to go into the chappel, and by prayer to call upon God for assistaunce. . . . . . He also buylded a great part of the east ende of the Guildhall, besyde many other good workes that I knowe not. But among all other I will shewe unto you one very notable, which I receyved credibly by a writyng of his awne hande, which also he willed to be fixed as a schedule to his last will and testament, the contentes whereof was that he willed and commaunded his executors as they would aunswere before God at the day of the resurrection of all fleshe, that if they found any debtor of his that ought to him any money, that if he were not in their consciences well worth three tymes as much, and also out of the debt of other men, and well able to pay, that then they shoulde never demaund it, for he cleerely forgave it, and that they should put no man in sute for any debt due to him. Looke upon thys, ye aldermen, for it is a glorious glasse."

Stow writes as follows in his *Survey of London* on some of Whittington's good works :—

" Richard Whittington, mercer, three times mayor, in the year 1421 began the library of the grey friars in London, to the charge of four hundred pounds : his executors with his goods founded and built Whittington College, with almshouses for thirteen poor men, and divinity lectures to be read there for ever. They repaired St. Bartholomew's hospital in Smithfield ; they bare half the charges of building the library there, and they built the west gate of London, of old time called Newgate," &c.*

* *Survey of London*, ed. Thoms, 1842, p. 41.

"The 1st year of Henry VI. John Coventrie and John Carpenter, executors to Richard Whitington, gave towards the paving of this great hall twenty pounds, and the next year fifteen pounds more, to the said pavement, with hard stone of Purbeck; they also glazed some windows thereof, and of the mayor's court; on every which windows the arms of Richard Whitington are placed." *

Respecting the library at Guildhall, Stow, after relating how the Duke of Somerset, Lord Protector, borrowed the books and never returned them, writes:—"This library was built by the executors of Richard Whittington and by William Burie; the arms of Whittington are placed on the one side in the stone work, and two letters, to wit W and B, for William Burie, on the other side; it is now lofted through, and made a storehouse for clothes." †

Whittington appears to have died childless, and in the interesting picture of his deathbed, copied by Mr. Lysons from an illumination in the ordinances of his college, his executors are seen around his bed. His will was proved in 1423 by John Coventry, John White, William Grove and John Carpenter. The College of St. Spirit and St. Mary consisted of a master, four fellows (masters of arts), clerks, conducts, chorists, &c. It was dissolved by Edward VI.; but the memory of it remains in the name College Hill, Upper Thames Street. God's House or Hospital for thirteen poor men was moved to Highgate in 1808.

* *Survey of London,* ed. Thoms, 1842, p. 162.   † *Ibid.* p. 103.

By his will Whittington directed that the inmates of his college should pray for the souls of himself and his wife Alice, of Sir William Whittington, and his wife Dame Joan, of Hugh Fitzwarren and his wife Dame Malde, as well as for the souls of Richard II. and Thomas of Woodstock, Duke of Gloucester, "special lords and promoters of the said Whittington."

Whittington's epitaph is preserved by Stow and is in Latin; yet the author of a *Life of Whittington* (1811) makes the following misstatement :—

"Record, however, has handed down to us the original epitaph, as it was cut on the monument of Sir Richard, by order of his executors; and, exclusive of its connection with the subject of these pages, it may be subjoined as a curious specimen of the poetry of an age which was comparatively with the present so entirely involved in the darkness of superstition and ignorance .

> "Beneath this stone lies Whittington,
>   Sir Richard rightly named ;
> Who three times Lord Mayor served in London,
>   In which he ne'er was blamed.
>
> He rose from indigence to wealth
>   By industry and that ;
> For lo! he scorned to gain by stealth
>   What he got by a cat.
>
> Let none who reads this verse despair
>   Of providences ways ;
> Who trust in him he'll make his care,
>   And prosper all their days.

Then sing a requiem to departed merit,
And rest in peace till death demands his spirit."—
Life of Sir R. Whittington, by the author of *Memoirs of George Barnwell*,
1811, p. 106.

LIST OF VERSIONS, EDITIONS, &c.

1604-5, Feb. 8. Play licensed, see *ante*, p. vii.

1605, July 16. Ballad licensed, see *ante*, p. vii.

1612. Johnson's Ballad published in *Crowne Garland of Goulden Roses*, see *ante*, p. ix.

1641? Roxburghe Ballad ("London's Glory"), see *ante*, p. xiv.

1670? Famous and Remarkable History by T. H., reprinted in this volume (see p. 1).

1678. Another edition with the same title as the above (see p. 1), but with the following imprint :

"London : Printed by A. P. and T. H. for T. Vere and J. Wright, and are to be sold at their shops at the Angel without Newgate and at the Crown on Ludgate Hill. 1678."

There are a few alterations in spelling, &c. but otherwise it is the same as the earlier edition.

1730. The History of Sir Richard Whittington, thrice Lord Mayor of London. Durham : Printed and sold by I. Lane.

This is the earliest version of the common chap-book tale in the British Museum. It is divided into chapters, and the headings of these chapters are given at p. xxx. of the present preface.   All the other chap-books that I have seen are more or less versions of this story, but one of the most complete is that printed in this Introduction (p. xxxii.)   The book was printed in most of the chief towns, as Newcastle, Edinburgh, &c. but one of the most interesting editions is that printed at York and illustrated by Bewick :—

The History of Whittington and his Cat; how from a poor country boy destitute of parents or relatives he attained great riches and was promoted to the high and honorable dignity of Lord Mayor of London.   York : Printed by J. Kendrew, Colliergate.

The frontispiece represents the stiff figure of a man in wig and gown of the time of Charles II., underneath which is printed —

> " Sir Richard Whittington behold
> In mayor's robes and chain of gold."

1808. In the *Antiquarian Repertory* (vol. ii. pp. 343-346) there is a good account of Whittington.

1811. The Life of Sir Richard Whittington, Knight, and four times Lord Mayor of London, in the reigns of Edward III. Richard II. and Henry V. Compiled from authentic documents; and containing many important particulars respecting that illustrious man never before published : intended to amuse, instruct, and stimulate the rising generation. By the Author of "Memoirs of George Barnwell." Harlow: Printed by B. Flower for M. Jones, No. 5, Newgate Street, London. 1811. Small 8vo.

1828. The Life of Sir Richard Whittington, Knight, four times Lord Mayor of London   London: Published by Thomas North, 64, Paternoster Row. 1828. (Lysons.)

1841. The Life and Times of Dick Whittington: an Historical Romance. London: Hugh Cuningham, St. Martin's Place. 1841. 8vo.

This is a novel written in imitation of Ainsworth, illustrated with plates in imitation of Cruikshank.

[1845.] Woodcock's "Lives of Illustrious Lords Mayors and Aldermen of London, with a Brief History of the City of London. London. 8vo. Pp. 28-46, Life of Whittington; but it contains no information of any value.

1860. The Model Merchant of the Middle Ages, exemplified in the Story of Whittington and his Cat: being an attempt to rescue that interesting story from the region of fable, and to place it in its proper position in the legitimate history of this country. By the Rev. Samuel Lysons, M.A. London: Hamilton, Adams & Co. 1860. 8vo.

1871. The Story of Sir Richard Whittington, Lord Mayor of London in the years 1397, 1406-7, and 1419 A.D. Written and illustrated by Carr. London: Longmans, Green and Co. 1871. Folio.

A new Ballad prettily illustrated, in which Canon Lysons's researches are taken into account, and the boy is made of good parentage, but the rest of the legend is retained.

1881. Sir Richard Whittington, Lord Mayor of London. By Walter Besant and James Rice. London: Marcus Ward and Co. 1881. Sm. 8vo.

Whittington and his Cat. By Ernest J. Miller. Published by the Albany Institute, Albany, N.Y. Weed, Parsons, and Company. 1881. 8vo.

A valuable paper, which contains a great mass of information on both the true and——the fictitious Whittington.

Whittington and his Cat, an Entertainment for Young People, by Miss Corner.

The Remarkable History of Richard Whittington and his Cat. Aunt Busy Bee's New Series. Dean and Son. Coloured illustrations on the page.

The following title is taken from Mr. Lysons's book, and I presume it is merely an edition of the ordinary chap-book.

History of Sir Richard Whittington. Printed at Sympson's in Stonecutter Street, Fleet Market.

The following extract from Granger's *History of England* is curious, as showing that the public would not have a portrait of Whittington without a representation of his famous cat :—

"The true portraicture of Richard Whitington, thrise Lord Maior of London; a vertuous and godly man, full of good works, and those famous. He builded the gate of London called Newegate, which before was a miserable doungeon. He builded Whitington College, and made it an almose-house for poore people. Also he builded a great parte of the hospitall of St. Bartholomew's, in West Smithfield, in London. He also builded the beautiful library at the Grey Friars in London, called Christe's Hospitall. He also builded the Guildehalle chappell, and increased a great parte of the east ende of the said halle, beside many other good workes."— *R. Elstracke sc. Collar of SS.; bis right band on a cat.*

Granger says of this :

"The cat has been inserted as the common people did not care to buy the print without it. There was none originally in the plate, but a skull in the place of the cat. I have seen only two proofs of this portrait in its first state, and these were fine impressions."—1775, vol. i. p. 62.

The following is a copy of the headings of the chapters in an early form of the chapbook version of Whittington's life :

THE

HISTORY

OF

SIR RICHARD WHITTINGTON,

THRICE LORD MAYOR OF LONDON.

Durham: Printed and sold by I. Lane. [1730.]

THE LIFE OF

SIR RICHARD WHITTINGTON.

Chap. I.

How, Whittington, being born of unknown parents, was left to a desperate fortune, and rambled the country till necessity and fear made him come to London.

Chap. II.

How, at the instance of Mrs. Alice, the Merchant's daughter, he became a servant in the family under the cook maid, who used him cruelly, and how Mrs. Alice took pity on him, and interpos'd her authority.

Chap. III.

How, lying in a garret, he was ready to be devoured by rats and mice, and to prevent it purchased a cat with a penny given him for cleaning shoes; and how, with the servants, he adventured the cat, being all his stock.

Chap. IV.

How the bitter jade of a cook maid encreasing her cruelty towards him he grew weary of his service, and was running away on All-Hallow's day; but upon hearing the ringing of Bow bells came back again. Also how the merchant abroad disposed of his cat.

Chap. V.

Of the great riches received for Whittington's cat more than for all the goods in the ship; on the arrival of which his master sent for him upstairs by the title of Mr. Whittington, and the excuses he made, and how he distributed part of his wealth to his fellow-servants giving the ill-natur'd cook maid 100*l*.

Chap. VI.

How Mr. Whittington, being genteely dress'd, became, to all appearance, a very comely, proper person; how Mrs. Alice, his master's daughter, fell in love with him, and, by her father's consent, married him; and also how he was chosen sheriff of London.

Chap. VII.

How he was thrice elected Lord Mayor of London; how he entertain'd King Henry. V. in his return from the conquest of France: with an account of his buildings for pious and charitable uses, great liberality to the poor, his death, burial, and epitaph.

EPITAPH.

Here lies Sir Richard Whittington, thrice mayor,
And his dear wife, a virtuous, loving pair;
Him fortune rais'd to be belov'd and great,
By the adventure only of a cat.
Let none who read of God's great love despair,
Who trusts in Him of him He will take care;
But growing rich chuse humbleness, not pride,
Let these dead persons' virtues be your guide.

The following reprint of a later version of the chap-
almost identical with a large number of editions :

THE

ADVENTURES

OF

SIR RICHARD WHITTINGTON,

WHO WAS

THREE TIMES

LORD MAYOR OF LONDON.

And the Surprising History of his

. CAT,

TO WHICH IS ADDED

THE CALEDONIAN, A POEM.

Banbury :
Printed and sold by J. Cheney, in the High Street.

THE

HISTORY

OF

WHITTINGTON.

Dick Whittington was a very little boy when his f
mother died ; little indeed, that he never knew them, nor

where he was born. He strolled about the country as ragged as a colt, till he met with a waggoner who was going to London, and who gave him leave to walk all the way by the side of his waggon without paying anything for his passage, which pleased little Whittington very much, as he wanted to see London sadly, for he had heard that the streets were paved with gold, and he was willing to get a bushel of it; but how great was his disappointment, poor boy! when he saw the streets covered with dirt instead of gold, and found himself in a strange place, without a friend, without food, and without money.

Though the waggoner was so charitable as to let him walk up by the side of the waggon for nothing, he took care not to know him when he came to town, and the poor boy was, in a little time, so cold and so hungry that he wished himself in a good kitchen and by a warm fire in the country.

In this distress he asked charity of several people, and one of them bid him "Go to work for an idle rogue." "That I will," says Whittington, "with all my heart; I will work for you if you will let me."

The man, who thought this favoured of wit and impertinence (tho' the poor lad intended only to show his readiness to work), gave him a blow with a stick which broke his head so that the blood ran down. In this situation, and fainting for want of food, he laid himself down at the door of one Mr. Fitzwarren, a merchant, where the cook saw him, and, being an ill-natured hussey, ordered him to go about his business or she would scald him. At this time Mr. Fitzwarren came from the Exchange, and began also to scold at the poor boy, bidding him to go to work.

Whittington answered that he should be glad to work if any

body would employ him, and that he should be able if he could get some victuals to eat, for he had had nothing for three days, and he was a poor country boy, and knew nobody, and nobody would employ him.

He then endeavoured to get up, but he was so very weak that he fell down again, which excited so much compassion in the merchant that he ordered the servants to take him in and give him some meat and drink, and let him help the cook to do any dirty work that she had to set him about. People are too apt to reproach those who beg with being idle, but give themselves no concern to put them in the way of getting business to do, or considering whether they are able to do it, which is not charity.

> " Think of this ye affluent,
> And when the overplus of your fortunes disturb
> Your minds, think how little stops the lash of penury,
> And makes the wretched happy ! "

I remember a circumstance of this sort, which Sir William Thompson told my father with tears in his eyes, and it is so affecting that I shall never forget it :

STORY
OF
SIR WILLIAM THOMPSON.

" When Sir William Thompson was in the plantation abroad, one of his friends told him he had an indentured servant whom he had just bought, that was his countryman and a lusty man ; ' but he is so idle,' says he, ' that I cannot get him to work.' ' Aye,' says Sir William, ' let me see him.' Accordingly they walked out together and found the man sitting on a heap of stones. Upon this Sir William, after enquiring about his country, asked why he did not go out to work.. 'I am not able,' answered the man. ' Not able ?' says Sir William, ' I am sure you look very well ; give him a few stripes.' Upon this the planter struck him several times, but the poor man still kept his seat.

Then they left him to look over the plantation, exclaiming against his obstinacy all the way they went ; but how surprised were they, on their return, to find the poor man fallen from off the place where he had been sitting, and dead !.. 'The cruelty,' says Sir William, ' of my ordering the poor man to be beaten while in the agonies of death lies always next my heart. It is what I shall never forget, and will for ever prevent my judging rashly of people who appear in distress. How do we know what our children may come to ? The Lord have mercy upon the poor, and defend them from the proud, the inconsiderate, and the avaricious." ..

But we return to Whittington : who would have lived happy in this worthy family had he not been bumped about by the cross cook, who must be always roasting or basting, and when the spit was still employed her hands upon poor Whittington ! till Miss Alice, his master's daughter, was informed of it, and then she took compassion on the poor boy, and made the servants treat him kindly.

Besides the crossness of the cook, Whittington had another difficulty to get over before he could be happy. He had, by order of his master, a flock-bed placed for him in a garret, where there were such a number of rats and mice that often ran over the poor boy's nose and disturbed him in his sleep. After some time, how-ever, a gentleman, who came to his master's house, gave Whittington a penny for brushing his shoes. This he put into his pocket, being determined to lay it out to the best advantage ; and the next day, seeing a woman in the street with a cat under her arm, he ran up to know the price of it. The woman (as the cat was a good mouser) asked a deal of money for it, but on Whittington's telling her he had but a penny in the world, and that he wanted a cat sadly, she let him have it.

This cat Whittington concealed in the garret, for fear she should be beat about by his mortal enemy the cook, and here she soon killed or frightened away the rats and mice, so that the poor boy could now sleep as sound as a top.

Soon after this the merchant, who had a ship ready to sail, called for his servants, as his custom was, in order that each of them might venture something to try their luck ; and whatever they sent was to pay neither freight nor custom, for he thought justly that God Almighty would bless him the more for his readiness to let the poor partake of his fortune. "He that giveth to the poor lendeth to the Lord, who will return it seventy-fold."

All the servants appeared but poor Whittington, who, having neither money nor goods, could not think of sending anything to try his luck ; but his good friend Miss Alice, thinking his poverty kept him away, ordered him to be called.

She then offered to lay down something for him, but the merchant told his daughter that would not do, it must be something of his own. Upon which poor Whittington said he had nothing but a cat which he bought for a penny that was given him. "Fetch thy cat, boy," said the merchant, "and send her." Whittington brought poor puss and delivered her to the captain, with tears in his eyes, for he said he should now be disturbed by the rats and mice as much as ever. All the company laughed at the adventure but Miss Alice, who pitied the poor boy, and gave him something to buy another cat.

While puss was beating the billows at sea, poor Whittington was severely beaten at home by his tyrannical mistress the cook, who used him so cruelly, and made such game of him for sending his cat to sea, that at last the poor boy determined to run away from his place, and, having packed up the few things he had, he set out very early in the morning on All-Hallows day. He travelled as far as Holloway, and there sat down on a stone to consider what course he should take ; but while he was thus ruminating, Bow bells, of which there were only six, began to ring ; and he thought their sounds addressed him in this manner :

> " Turn again, Whittington,
> Lord Mayor of great London."

"Lord Mayor of London !" said he to himself; " what would not one endure to be Lord Mayor of London, and ride in such a fine coach ? Well, I'll go back again, and bear all the pummelling and ill-usage of Cicely rather than miss the opportunity of being Lord Mayor !" So home he went, and happily got into the house and about his business before Mrs. Cicely made her appearance.

We must now follow Miss Puss to the coast of Africa, to that coast where Dido expired for loss of Ænus *(sic).* How perilous are voyages at sea, how uncertain the winds and the waves, and how many accidents attend a naval life !

The ship, which had the cat on board, was long beaten at sea, and at last, by contrary winds, driven on a part of the coast of Barbary which was inhabited by Moors, unknown to the English. These people received our countrymen with civility, and therefore the captain, in order to trade with them, shewed them the patterns of the goods he had on board, and sent some of them to the king of the country, who was so well pleased that he sent for the captain and the factor to his palace, which was about a mile from the sea. Here they were placed, according to the custom of the country, on rich carpets, flowered with gold and silver; and the king and queen being seated at the upper end of the room, dinner was brought in, which consisted of many dishes; but no sooner were the dishes put down but an amazing number of rats and mice came from all quarters, and devoured all the meat in an instant. The factor, in surprise, turned round to the nobles and asked " If these vermin were not offensive?" " O yes," said they, " very offensive; and the king would give half his treasure to be freed of them, for they not only destroy his dinner, as you see, but they assault him in his chamber, and even in bed, so that he is obliged to be watched while he is sleeping for fear of them."

The factor jumped for joy; he remembered poor Whittington and his cat, and told the king he had a creature on board the ship that would despatch all these vermin immediately. The king's heart heaved so high at the joy which this news gave him that his turban dropped off his head. " Bring this creature to me," says he; " vermin are dreadful in a court, and if she will perform what you say, I will load your ship with gold and jewels in exchange for her." The factor, who knew his business, took this opportunity to set forth the merits of Miss Puss. He told his majesty " That it would be inconvenient to part with her, as, when she was gone, the rats and mice might destroy the goods in the ship—but to oblige his majesty he would fetch her." " Run, run," said the queen; " I am impatient to see the dear creature."

Away flew the factor, while another dinner was providing, and returned with the cat just as the rats and mice were devouring that also. He immediately put down Mrs. Puss, who killed a great number of them.

The king rejoiced greatly to see his old enemies destroyed by so small a creature, and the queen was highly pleased, and desired the cat might he brought near that she might look at her. Upon which the factor called " Pussy, pussy, pussy," and she came to him. He then presented her to the queen, who started back, and was afraid to touch a creature who had made such a havoc among the rats and mice ; however, when the factor stroked the cat and called " Pussy, pussy," the queen also touched her and cried " Putty, putty," for she had not learned English.

He then put her down on the queen's lap, where she, purring, played with her majesty's hand, and then sung herself to sleep.

The king having seen the exploits of Mrs. Puss, and being informed that she was with young, and would stock the whole country, bargained with the captain and factor for the whole ship's cargo, and then gave them ten times as much for the cat as all the rest amounted to. With which, taking leave of their majesties, and other great personages at court, they sailed with a fair wind for England, whither we must now attend them.

The morn had scarcely dawned when Mr. Fitzwarren stole from the bed of his beloved wife, to count over the cash, and settle the business for that day. He had just entered the compting-house, and seated himself at the desk, when somebody came, tap, tap, at the door. " Who's there ?" says Mr. Fitzwarren. " A friend," answered the other. " What friend can come at this unseasonable time ?" " A real friend is never unseasonable," answered the other. "I come to bring you good news of your ship *Unicorn.*" The merchant bustled up in such an hurry that he forgot his gout; instantly opened the door, and who should be seen waiting but the captain and factor, with a cabinet of jewels, and a bill of lading, for which the merchant lifted up his eyes and thanked heaven for sending him such a prosperous voyage. Then they told him the adventures of the cat, and shewed him the cabinet of jewels which they had brought for Mr. Whittington. Upon which he cried out with great earnestness, but not in the most poetical manner,—

> "Go, send him in, and tell him of his fame,
> And call him Mr. Whittington by name."

It is not our business to animadvert upon these lines; we are not critics, but historians. It is sufficient for us that they are the words of Mr. Fitzwarren; and though it is beside our purpose, and perhaps not in our power to prove him a good poet, we shall soon convince the reader that he was a good man, which was a much better character; for when some, who were present, told him that this treasure was too much for such a poor boy as Whittington, he said, "God forbid that I should deprive him of a penny; it is his own, and he shall have it to a farthing." He then ordered Mr. Whittington in, who was at this time cleaning the kitchen, and would have excused himself from going into the compting-house, saying, the room was rubbed, and his shoes were dirty and full of hob-nails. The merchant, however, made him come in, and ordered a chair to be set for him. Upon which, thinking they intended to make sport of him, as had been too often the case in the kitchen, he besought his master not to mock a poor simple fellow, who intended them no harm, but let him go about his business. The merchant, taking him by the hand, said, "Indeed,

Mr. Whittington, I am in earnest with you, and sent for you to congratulate you on your great success. Your cat has procured you more money than I am worth in the world, and may you long enjoy it and be happy."

At length, being shown the treasure, and convinced by them that all of it belonged to him, he fell upon his knees and thanked the Almighty for his providential care of such a poor and miserable creature. He then laid all the treasure at his master's feet, who refused to take any part of it, but told him he heartily rejoiced at his prosperity, and hoped the wealth he had acquired would be a comfort to him, and would make him happy. He then applied to his mistress, and to his good friend Miss Alice, who refused to take any part of the money, but told him she heartily rejoiced at his good success, and wished him all imaginable felicity. He then gratified the captain, factor, and the ship's crew, for the care they had taken of his cargo. He likewise distributed presents to all the servants in the house, not forgetting even his old enemy the cook, though she little deserved it.

After this Mr. Fitzwarren advised Mr. Whittington to send for the necessary people and dress himself like a gentleman, and made him the offer of his house to live in till he could provide himself with a better.

Now it came to pass that when Mr. Whittington's face was washed, his hair curled, and dressed in a rich suit of clothes, that he turned out a genteel young fellow; and, as wealth contributes much to give a man confidence, he in a little time dropped that sheepish behaviour which was principally occasioned by a depression of spirits, and soon grew a sprightly and good companion, insomuch that Miss Alice, who had formerly seen him with an eye of compassion, now viewed him with other eyes, which perhaps was in some measure occasioned by his readiness to oblige her, and by continually making her presents of such things that he thought would be most agreeable.

When her father perceived they had this good liking for each other he proposed a match between them, to which both parties cheerfully consented, and the Lord Mayor, Court of Aldermen, Sheriffs, the Company of Stationers, and a number of eminent merchants attended the ceremony, and were elegantly treated at an entertainment made for that purpose.

History further relates that they lived very happy, had several children, and died at a good old age. Mr. Whittington served Sheriff of London in the year 1340, and was three times Lord Mayor. In the last year of his mayoralty he entertained King Henry V. and his Queen, after his conquest of France, upon which occasion the King, in consideration of Whittington's merit, said, "Never had prince such a subject;" which being told to Whittington at the table, he replied "Never had subject such a king." His Majesty, out of respect to his good character, conferred the honour of knighthood on him soon after.

Sir Richard many years before his death constantly fed a great number of poor citizens, built a church and a college to it, with a yearly allowance for poor scholars, and near it erected an hospital. He also built Newgate for criminals, and gave liberally to St. Bartholomew's Hospital and other public charities.

Two old houses in London, which were pulled down at the beginning of the present century, have been associated with the name of Whittington, but there is no evidence that he really dwelt in either of them. One ruinous building in Sweedon's Passage, Grub Street, engravings of which will be found in J. T. Smith's *Topography of London*, was pulled down in 1805, and five houses built on its site. A tablet was then set up, on which was an inscription to the effect that the house had been called Gresham House, and that Whittington once inhabited it.

The magnificent house which stood in Hart Street, Crutched Friars, a few doors from Mark Lane, is said to have been called Whittington's palace in the old leases, but this is the only evidence in favour of the popular belief. The front was elaborately carved in oak, the work of a much later date than that of Whittington. The decoration is attributed to the latter part of the reign of Henry VIII., and on the ceiling among other forms was that of a cat's head, from which possibly the tradition of its having been the residence of Whittington arose. There was a popular superstition that the cat's eyes followed the visitor as he walked about the room. This house was taken down in 1801, but both it and the house in Sweedon's Passage were reproduced in the interesting Old London Street at the International Health Exhibition of 1884.

THE

FAMOUS AND REMARKABLE

HISTORY

OF

SIR RICHARD WHITTINGTON,

THREE TIMES LORD MAYOR OF LONDON:

who lived in the time of King Henry the Fifth in the year 1419, *with*
all the Remarkable Passages, and things of note, which hap-
pened in his time: with his Life and Death.

WRITTEN BY T. H.

———————

Printed by W. Thackeray and T. Passinger.

The Printer to the Reader.

Courteous Reader,—I here present unto thee no strange or forreign news, no imagination, or vain conceit of poetical fiction; neither do I tell thee of Gallagantua or of the Red Rose Knight, nor such like stories; but I here offer to thy view a true pattern of humility; being the glory of our Kingdom, and raised to Honour by desert; the title tells you that it is the life and death of Richard Whittington, who for his clemency and understanding was three times chosen Lord Mayor of the Honourable City of London, who always acknowledged his beginning to be of mean and low rank; yet he was beloved of the King for his fidelity and trust, as may appear in larger volumes, and the entertainment that he gave at his own house to his Soveraign at several times : his bounty upon all occasions, when the King wanted his purse; his love to the City and Commons; which are not to be buried in oblivion, but rather to be proclaimed as living monuments to all people of what condition soever, to animate them never to be dejected though never so poor, as the story will more at large declare; all which happened in the days of our forefathers, and very probable it may be for us to believe; if we will not give credit to former historians who will give the like to us in future ages: read it through, and you will find something worthy of note, and thou shall do thy self some pleasure and me a high favour. *Vale.*

The Life and Death of Sir Richard Whittington; who was three times Lord Mayor of the City of London.

The saying is not so old as true, He that refuseth to buy counsel cheap shall buy repentance dear; neither let any work [mock?] a man in his misery, but rather beware by him how to avoid the like misfortune; if thou intend to do any good, defer it not till the next day, for thou knowest not what may happen over night to prevent thee. Behold thyself in a looking glass, if thou appearest beautiful do such things as may become thy beauty; but if thou seem foul or deformed, let the actions of thy life make good that splendor which thy face lacketh. Tell not thy mind to every man, make thy self indebted to no man, be friend to few men, be courteous to all men, let thy wit be thy friend, thy mind thy companion, thy tongue thy servant, let vertue be thy life, valour thy love, honour thy fame and heaven thy felicity. These (Reader) be good documents for thee to follow, and I am now to present thee with a worthy

president to imitate; observe his beginning, forget not the
middle passage of his life, and thou wilt no question crown his
head.   He that made all things of nothing can of a little make
much, and multiply a mite into a magazine, as will easily
appear by the succeeding history.

   This Richard Whittington was so obscurely born that he
could scarcely give account of his parents or kindred, and being
almost starved in the country, necessity compelled him up to
London, hoping to find more charity in the town than in the
country: to beg he was ashamed, to steal he did abhor: two
days he spent in gaping upon the shops and gazing upon the
buildings feeding his eyes but starving his stomach.   At length
meer faintness compell'd him to rest himself upon a bench
before a merchant's gate, where he not long sat but the owner
of the house having occasion of business into the town finding
him a poor simple fellow, and thinking that he had no more
within him than appeared without, demanded of him why he
loytered there, and being able to work for his living did not
apply himself unto some lawful calling, threatning him at the
first with the stocks and the whipping-post; but the poor man,
after the making of some plain leggs and courtesie, desired him
to pardon him, and told him that he was a dejected man, who
desired any imployment, and that no pains how mean or course
(*sic*) soever could seem tedious or burthensome unto him, so he
might but find some good master, by whose charity he might
relieve his present necessity: for his great ambition was but to

keep his body from nakedness and his stomach from hunger, and told him withal how long it was since he had tasted meat or drink.

The worthy merchant seeing him of a personable body, and an ingenious aspect howsoever both were clouded under a rustick habit, began somewhat to commiserate his estate, and knocking for a servant had him take in that fellow and give him such victuals as the house for the present afforded, and at his return he would have further conference with him. The servant did as he was commanded and took him in.

The merchant went then to the Exchange, which was then in Lumber Street, about his affairs; in which intrim (*sic*) poor Whittington was hied into the kitchin to warm himself, for faintness by reason of hunger and cold (for it was then in the winter time) had quite rob'd him of his colour. Meat was set before him in plenty, and being bred in the country, as the proverb goeth, *He fed like a farmer,* and having satisfied himself sufficiently and warm'd him to the full, a fresh colour began to come into his cheeks: at which the Merchant's daughter (hearing of a new come guest) came into the kitchin, and began to question him of divers things concerning the country, to all which he gave her such modest and sensible answers that she took a great liking unto him, and so left him.

Dinner time came, and Master Fitzwarren (for so was the merchant called) came home with a good stomach, and brought a friend or two with him from the Exchange; down they sat to meat, and had speech of many things at the table; meanwhile the servants were set also at dinner, who would needs have Whittington, though he had so lately broke his fast, to keep them company, some of them delighting in his country speech, others deriding his supposed simplicity.

But to come to the purpose, the table being withdrawn in the parlour, and the guests departed, and Master Fitzwarren and his daughter left alone, she being of a good and gentle disposition, began to commend his charity concerning the poor man whom he relieved that morning, to whom he answered, God-a-mercy daughter, thou hast done well to remember me, such a one I sent indeed, but have my servants done as I commanded them? and where is he now? who answered him, that she had given order he should stay dinner, and not depart the house till he himself had further spoken with him. At which they both went unto the Hall, and called the fellow before them; who appeared unto them with such a bashful humility that it seemed to them both to beg a charity; some language past betwixt them concerning him, which gave them content; at length they bid him retire himself.

When the father and the daughter had some private conference concerning him she urged him to entertain him into his house, and that there would be some employment for him, either to run or to go of errands or else to do some drudgery in the kitchin, as making of fires, scouring kettles, turning the spit, and the like: To whom the father reply'd that indeed his work might be worth his meat, but he had no lodging to spare, and she again answered that there were garrets in the house that were put to no use at all, and in one of them he might conveniently be lodged and put the house to no trouble at all.

Well at length he was admitted, and made a member of the family, in which he demeaned himself so well by his willingness to run or go or do any service how mean so ever that he had got the good will of all the whole houshold, only the kitchin maid being a curst quean, and knowing him to be an under servant to her, domineered over him and used him very coursely and roughly, of which he would never complain, though he had cause enough. The garret in which he lay, by reason it had been long unfrequented, was troubled with rats and mice, insomuch that he could not sleep in the night but they ran over his face, and much disturb'd him in his rest: to prevent which having got a penny either for going of an errand, or for making clean boots or shooes or the like, with that he bought a young cat which he kept in his garret, and whatsoever he had from the reversion of the servants table he would be sure to reserve part for her, because he had found by experience that she had rid him of the former inconveniences.

The History tells us that this merchant, Master Hugh Fitz-warren, was so generous that he never adventured any ship to sea but he would have his daughter, his cashire, and every one

B

of his servants, whar (*sic*) or whatsoever, to put in something, and to adventure with him, and according to that proportion which they could spare, every one received to a token at the return of the ship.   His daughter she began, the rest followed, and the servants borrowed out of their wages everyone according to their abilities, and when they all had done Whittington was remembered and called for, and his master telling him the custome of his home, asked him what he had to hazard in this adventure.   who replyed again, he was a poor man, and had nothing in the world saving the cloaths upon his back, but for money he had none at all : then his daughter drew out her purse and told her father, that for his servant Whittington she would lay down whatsoever he would desire.   Who answered again, that what she had spoke was nothing to the purpose; for whatsoever was ventured in that kind must be out of ones proper goods and chattels, and again demanded of him if he had anything he could call his own to put to hazard, and charged him deeply concerning that point, who making some unnecessary leggs, told him that he had nothing which he could call his saving a cat, which he had bought with his penny, which he could not spare because she had done him so many good offices, and told them every circumstance before related, which when the merchant heard he told him that he should venture that commodity and none else, and charged him to fetch her instantly (for the ship which was called the Unicorn) was fallen down as low as Blackwal and all their lading was already had aboard. Whittington although unwilling to part from so good a companion yet being forced by his masters command by whom he had his subsistence he brought her and (not without tears) delivered her to his factor who was partly glad of her, by reason they were troubled with mice and rats in the ship, which not only spoyled their victuals but damaged their wares and commodities.

I must leave the cat upon her voyage at sea and honest Whittington on land, who by that cursed quean the kitchin maid was so beaten and abused that he was as weary of his life as of his service: for she (usurping upon his plainness and modesty) would be quarrelling with him, upon every small or no occasion at all; sometimes beating him with the broom, sometimes laying him over the shoulders with a laddle, the spit or what came next to her hands, being of so dogged a disposition that she still continued her cruelty towards him, and therefore he resolved with himself to run away, and for that purpose he had bundled up those few clothes which he had, and before day broke was got as far as Bun-hill, and then he sat down to consider with himself what course he were best to take; where by chance (it being all-hallows day) a merry peal from Bow Church began to ring, and as he apprehended they were tun'd to this ditty,—

Turn again Whittington, Lord Mayor of London,
Turn again Whittington, Lord Mayor of London.

This took such a great impression in him, that finding how early it was, and that he might yet come back in his masters house before any of the family were stirring, he resolved to go back, and found every thing according to his own wishes and desires, insomuch that when the household were up none could challenge him to have been missing. And thus he continued as before in his first plainness and honesty, well beloved of all save the kitchin drudge; I come now to tell you what became of his adventure.

It so hapned that this goodly ship Unicorn was by contrary gusts and bad weather driven upon the utmost coast of Barbary, where never any Englishman (or scarce any Christian) had ever traded before, where they showed their commodities and offered them to be vended. The Moors came down in multitudes, much taken with the beauty of their ship, for they had never seen any of that bigness or burthen before, but when they had taken a serious view of their commodities as hatchets, knives and looking-glasses, fish-hooks, &c. but especially their cloth and kersies of several sizes and colours, they brought them gold in abundance for it was more plentiful with them then *(sic)* lead or copper with us.

Presently the news was carryed to the king who sent some of his chief nobility to bring him some sorts of every commodity that was aboard, which when he saw they pleased him highly, sending for the master and merchants factor to court.

He at their own rate bargained with them for their whole lading, nor would he suffer them to depart till he had feasted them royally.

Now the fashion of the Moors is not to sit at the table as the custom is among us, but to have a rich carpet spread upon the ground, and when the meal or banquet is served in, as well the king himself as the rest sit round about cross-legg'd as taylors commonly used to do upon their shop-boards, and in that manner our English are set at the king's banquet, but the meal was no sooner served in but swarms of rats and mice seized upon the dishes, and snatched away the meat even from the king and queen's trenchers: at which the factor being annoyed asked one of the nobility (by an interpreter) if they preserved those vermin for sport, or if they were noysome, and troublesome unto them: who answered him again, that they were the greatest vexation unto them that could be possible, and by reason of their multitudes they could not be destroyed, but the king would willingly give half the revenue of his crown if he could but only clear the court of them, for not only his table but his very bed-chamber swarmed with them, insomuch that he durst not lay him down to rest without a watch about him, to keep them off his pillow: To whom the factor replyed, that they had a strange beast aboard which he made no doubt would rid them of those vermine: which being told the king he rose from his place and imbracing the factor told him if he could shew him such a creature he would ballast his vessel with silver and lade her with gold and pearl. Who apprehending the occasion made very coy of the business, telling him it was a creature of great value and not common. Besides they could not spare her from the ship, in regard when they were asleep yet she was still waking in the night, not only to preserve their merchandise but there dyet from the like spoyl. The more dainty that he made of the matter the more earnest was the king for this beast, insomuch that he was presently sent for.

And a second feast being prepared and the rats and mice appearing as they did before, the young merchant having the cat under his cloak the king desired to see the thing which he had before so much commended; when presently he discovered her, and cast her among them; she no sooner saw these vermine but fell upon them with such a fury that here lay one panting, there another quite dead ; nor left them till she had frighted and disperst the whole number, but such as she seized their carkasses lay there as witnesses of their unexpected slaughter.

Great pleasure took the king and the nobility in the sport, vowing that the hunting of the lyon (of which there was plenty in that country) was not answerable unto it. In the interim one began to praise her for her colour, another commending her for her valour, one said she had the countenance of a lyon, and every one gave his sentence. When the poor cat finding no more work for her to do, went round to the King and Queen purling and curling (as their manner is), which they apprehended to be, as if she inquired of them what she had deserved for that late service.

To cut off circumstance, no price could part them, and the rather when the factor had told the king that she was with kittens, and that her brood would in some few years, being carefully lookt into, furnish the whole kingdom, so that Whittingtons cats adventure only surmounted all the ships lading beside, with which fortune and unexpected gain we bring them safe into England; the ship lying at anchor near Blackwal, and the Pilot and Cape-merchant, with some other officers in the ship at Mr. Fitzwarrens house, which was by Leaden-Hall, to give accompt of their voyage. But these caskets of jewels and pearls, with other unvaluable (*sic*) riches which were given for the cat, they caused to be brought along, not daring, by reason of their inestimable value, to trust them in the ship. The Bills of lading and the benefit of the return of the Commodities being viewed and considered of by the owner, he praised God for so prosperous a voyage, and called all his servants and gave order that according to their adventures every one should receive his portion.

At length casting his eye upon those rich caskets and cabinets, he asked to whose share they belonged; who whispered him in the ear, and told him to his poor Whittington, relating every particular as is before discoursed. To whom Master Fitz-warren replyed, if they then be his, God forbid I should keep from him the least farthing that is his right, and presently commanded Whittington to be sent for by the name of Mr. Whittington.

The servants not knowing anything of the business, went unto him into the kitchin, where he was then rubbing the spits, scouring the kettles, and making clean the dressers, and told him he must come to his Master presently into the parlor. The poor man excused himself, that his shooes were dirty and the room was rubb'd, and if he should but touch any thing there he should spoyl and deface those things in the room. But still the master of the House called for Master Whittington, sending one servant after another till he was brought before him ; and having scraped some few legs, instantly his master took him by the hand, and called for a chair for Master Whittington, his daughter, the pilot, and the factor, every one of them saluted him by the name of Mr. Whittington and forced him to sit down. He wondering what this should mean desired them not to mock a poor simple man who meant none any harm, &c. and wept (the tears dropping from his eyes), desiring them not to deride his poverty, for his ambition was never to come so high as from the kitchin to the hall much more from the hall to the parlor.

Then came his master to him seriously and said, Indeed Mr. Whittington, we are all in very good earnest, for you are at this time a better man than myself in estate, and then shewed him all those cabinets and caskets, and how richly they were lined.

When he perceived by all their earnest asservations that all was true he first fell down upon his knees and gave God most hearty thanks, who out of his great bounty would vouchsafe to cast an eye upon so poor and wretched a creature as himself; then turning to his master he presented all his riches before him and told him that all he had was at his disposing and service, who answered him again, that for his own part God had sent him sufficient of his own, neither would he take from him the value of one Barbary ducket. He came nere and with a low leg saluted his mistris, and told her that when she pleased to make choice of a husband he would make her the richest marriage in London, because she was so willing out of her own purse (when he was altogether penniless) to lay out for his adventure. To the pilot, and master, and every officer, and common saylor he gave liberal according to their degree, even to the ship boy, and then to every servant of the house, nay to the very kitchin wench who was so churlish unto him, and had so often basted him instead of her roast meats; having caused her to be called unto him he gavé her an hundred pounds towards her marriage.

c

This being done, taylors were sent for, sempsters and the like to put him into cloaths and linnen of the best, who were to accommodate him with all speed possible, and his lodging in the garret was chang'd into the best chamber of the house. And when the barber had been with him and the rest to make him compleat in his habit, there was a strange and sudden metamorphosis; for out of a smoky and dirty kitchin-drudge there appeared a proper and well-proportioned man, and gentile merchant, in so much that his young mistris began to cast a more amorous eye upon him than before, which not a little pleased Master Fitzwarren her father, who intended a match betwixt them.

The brute of this great adventure was presently revised through the whole city, insomuch that his master intreated his late servant to walk with him into the Exchange to see the fashion of the merchants, which he did, when all of them came about him and saluted him, some bid God give him joy of his fortune, others desired of him better and further acquaintance, and every one as his several fancy led him: some commended him for his person, others for his modest answers and discreet carriage.   Indeed, wealth is able to make all these good where they are most wanting, which was not in him as appears by the sequel.

Within few weeks the match was propounded betwixt Master

Whittington and Mistris Alice, and willingly entertained by both parties and not without great cost, with the invitation of the Lord Mayor and the Aldermen very nobly celebrated, and the bridegroom by this means had got acquaintances with the best.

After this his father-in-law demanded of his son what he purposed to take in hand (his freedom being offered him). Who made answer again that since God had so blest him in his small adventure he would not leave it of so, but prove his goodness in a greater, and that his purpose was to turn merchant, which reply gave him no small content in regard he knew the best among them would be glad to have the society of so hopeful a citizen, which he continued adventuring in divers bottoms with his father, and had very happy and prosperous returns.

The time being come when he was prickt for Sheriff he modestly refused it as unable to take so great a charge, and would willingly have paid his fine, which his father-in-law would not suffer, at whose persuasion he took the place upon him, in which he so well behaved himself in the management of all affairs belonging to his office that he not only left it without the least taxation, but with a general love and approbation, insomuch that the universal eye of the whole city was fixt upon him in an hopeful expectation what a profitable member of that united body he might futurely prove, and this hapned in the year of our Lord 1493, Sir John Hodley grocer being mayor and Drewerie Barentine his fellow Sheriff, of the truth of which Mr. Fabian in his *Chronicle* and Mr. John Stow in his *Survey of London* can fully satisfie you.

In the year 1497 and the one and twentieth of the same Kings reign, Sir Richard Whittington was Lord Mayor of London, John Woodcok and William Askam being Sheriffs, and he held the place with great reputation and honour. In which time of his Mayoralty there was much discontent in the kingdom, by reason of many differences betwixt the King and the Commons; the circumstances whereof were here too long to relate, only one thing is worthy of observation that whether by his adventures or no may it be questioned, bringing in yearly such store of gold, silks, sattins, velvets, damasks, stones, and jewels, &c. into the kingdom might be the cause of that great pride and rioting in apparel which was used in those days. But as Harding, Fabian, and others have left to me how in that year of his Mayoralty and after there resorted to the Kings Court at their pleasures daily, at the least ten thousand persons. In his kitchin were three hundred servitors, and in every office according to that rate. Moreover of ladies, chambermaids, and laundresses about three hundred, and they all exceeded in gorgeous and costly apparel far above their degrees; for even the yeomen and grooms were clothed in silks and velvets, damasks, and the like, with imbroydery, rich furs, and goldsmiths work, devising very strange and new fashions.

And in this year also, about the feast of St. Bartholomew, grew a great discord betwixt the Duke of Hereford and Mowbery, Duke of Norfolk, the beginning thereof being as followeth: The two Dukes riding from the Parliament towards their lodgings, the Duke of Norfolk said to the other, Sir, you see how variable the King is in his words, and (reflecting upon what had past) how without mercy he putteth his Lords and kinsfolks to death, imprisoning some and exciting others. Therefore it behoveth us not too much to trust to his fair and smooth language, for doubtless in time he will bring even to us the like death and destruction. Of which words he accused him to the King, which the other denying it was to be tryed by combate. The lists were appointed and the day of meeting the eleventh day of September, to which place and on the day assigned came both the Dukes and bravely accoutred, appeared before the King ready to enter into battel; when the King threw down his warder, and staying the combate banished the Duke of Hereford for ten years, but the Duke of Norfolk for ever, was travelling many countries, at the last came to Venice and then ended his life.

Again in 1406, and in the eighth of Henry the fourth, Sir Richard Whittington was the second time Lord Mayor, Nicholas Worton and Geffery Brook being Sheriffs. Again in the year 1409, being the seventh year of Henry the fifth, he supplyed the Pretorship, Robert Whittington (his near Kinsman) and John Butler being Sheriffs, and which is more remarkable of him then of any other that ever preceded him in that place of honour, he was once Sheriff and three times Lord Mayor of this famous and honourable City in three several Kings reigns.

Now to cut off all circumstances and come close to the matter, we may easily find what this man was, by the pious and religious acts done in his life to the Cities present grace, use and benefit, and to his own blessed memory for ever.

In the Vintry-ward he built a church and dedicated it to S. Michael 'calling it Pater Noster in the Royal, and added to it a Colledge founded to St. Mary, and placed therein a President and four fellows which ought to be masters of arts, besides other yearly allowance to clerks and young schollars, near which he erected an Hospital which he called God's house, for thirteen poor men, and there according to the devout superstition of those days were to pray for the souls of his father-in-law Hugh Fitzwarren and Dame Molde his wife, for whom he erected a fair tomb in the church he before built, leaving also a place for himself and Dame Alice his lady when it should please God to call them. In which place they were afterwards both of them according to their degree very honourably interred, great mourning and much lamentation being made for him by the Commons of the City in regard he was a man so remarkable for his charity.

He builded another brave structure which he called after his own name Whittington Colledge, with a perpetual allowance for Divinity Lectures to be read there for ever, leaving good land for the maintenance thereof.

And on the west side of the City he built that famous gate and prison to this day called Newgate, and thereupon caused the Merchants arms to be graven in stone. He added to St. Bartholomew's Hospital in Smithfield and was at the charge of repairing thereof.

Further at the Grey-Fryars in London he erected a Library as a testimony of the great love he had to Learning, which he began in the year of our Lord 1421 and finished it in the year following. Moreover that place which is called the Stocks to this day, betwixt Cheapside and Cornhill, a good house of stone, which for a flesh market and a fish market greatly beneficial to the City.

Besides he enlarged Guild Hall and glazed most or all of the windows at his own costs or charges, paving the Hall and contributing largely to the Library, adding to those places a conduit which yieldeth store of sweet and wholesome water to the general good and benefit of the City.

In the year 1497, when Sir Richard Whittington was first elected Lord Mayor, that rebel Sir John Oldcastle was taken in the territories of the Lord Powess, not without danger and hurt of some that took him, at which time all the States of the realm were assembled at Parliament in London, therein to provide the King of a subsidy and other aid of money and ammunition, who took great pains beyond the seas in France. These Lords and others when they heard that the publick enemy was taken they agreed all not to dissolve the Parliament, until he were examined, and heard to answer in the same. Whereupon the Lord Powess was sent for to fetch him up with power and great aid, who brought him to London in a lyter wounded very much having received seventeen wounds and also a clerk which he called his Secretary with him that was of his counsel in all his secrecy. As soon as the aforesaid Sir John Oldcastle was brought into the Parliament before the Earl of Bedford who was then left Regent and Governour of the Realm in the time of the King's absence being in France and other Lords and States, his indictment being read before him of his forcible insurrection against the King and State in St. Gyles's Fields, and other treasons and outrages by him committed, the question was asked how he could excuse himself and show why he should not be judged to dye according to the law. But he seeking other talk and discourse of the mercies of God, and that all mortal men that would be followers of God ought to prefer mercy above judgment and that vengeance pertained only to the Lord, and ought not to be practised by them that worship, but to be left to God alone, with many other words to protract the time, until the Lord Chief Justice admonished the Regent not to suffer him to spend the time so vainly, in molesting the nobles of the Realm, whereupon the Duke of Bedford, Regent, commanded him to answer formally and punctually to the matter laid to his charge.

Then said Sir John, being thus urged at last after deliberation taken, he said, It is the least thing that I account of to be judged by you as of man's judgment, and again he began to talk, but nothing to the purpose until the Chief Justice commanded him again to answer finally, and to answer them if he could, why he should not suffer death according to his desert. To which he stoutly answered that he had no judge amongst them, so long as his liege Lord King Richard was alive and in his realm of Scotland, which answer when he had made, because there needed no further witness, he was then presently censured to be drawn and hanged on a gallows and then to be burnt hanging upon the same, which judgment was executed upon him the thirtieth day of December in St. Gyles's Fields, where many honourable persons were present, and the last words that he spake were to Sir Thomas Upingham, adjuring him that if he saw him rise from death to life again the third day he would procure that his sect which he had raised might be in peace and quiet. He was hanged by the neck in a chain of iron and after consumed by fire.

Moreover it is recorded that in the time of this worthy

D

pretor Sir Richard Whittington the glorious city of Constan-
tinople was taken by Mahomet the Second, Prince of the
Turks, whose souldiers sacked it with all extremity and
omitted no manners of cruelty by violence to either virgins,
aged women, or sucking babes. This Sir Richard Whittington had traffick from thence by his factors which there abode,
and were then taken prisoners, so that he lost near upon
fifteen thousand pounds, which when he heard of never was
so much as cast down or dismayed, but said God will send
more; yea such was the incessant practice of the Turkish
tyranny upon this imperial city, as it exceeded the damage,
rapes and spoyls of other cities. They also beheaded at the
same time Constantine, sticking his head upon a launce, and
with derision caused it to be carried thorow the Turkish camp.

In the space of a week after, there hapned a horrible tem-
pest of thunder and lightning which burned almost eight hundred houses and spoiled three thousand people at the sacking
of the aforesaid city by the said Mahomet. The Turks found
therein so much treasure that they wondred that the citizens
would not spend it in souldiers for their own defence, but so
dotingly to spare the true spending thereof to become an en-
ticing prey for their irreconcileable enemies, for indeed it was
thought that if the State would have hired souldiers, and given
them good pay they might have raised the siege of the Turks.
It is an old and true saying, Covetousness is the mother of
ruine and mischief.

This strange thing hapned in the second time that he was elected Lord Mayor and that was upon the twenty-seventh of April, being Tuesday in Easter week: William Foxley, Pot maker for the Mint in the Tower of London, fell asleep, and so continued sleeping and snoring and could not be wakened with pricking, cramping, or otherwise burning or whatsoever till the first day of the term, which was full 14 days and 15 nights. The cause of this his sleeping could not be known though the same was diligently searched for by the King's Command of his Physicians and other learned men, yea the King himself examined the said William Foxley, who was in all points sound at his awaking to be as if he had slept but one night, and yet lived 41 years after. But in length of time did call to mind how he did wish to God that he might sleep a fortnight together if it was not so and so concerning a bargain between a neighbour of his and himself.

One Thursday in Whitson week following the Duke of Somerset with Anthony Rivers and four others kept Justs and Tournament before the King and Queen and others of the nobility in the Tower of London, against three Esquires of the Queen's Bedchamber, which were performed before some of the French nobility that then were Prisoners to the King, which he took in France, to the great admiration of those strangers who never saw the like action before, being so earnestly performed. There was also Sir Richard Whittington and the two

Sheriffs, and that night the King and Queen did sup with the Lord Mayor.

Those strangers which beheld those Justs were prisoners in the Tower at that time, namely, the Duke of Orleance and Burbon, brother to the Duke of Britain, the Earls of Vaudosine, of Ewe and Richmond, and the High Marshal of France, and many other Knights and Esquires to the number of seven hundred, all which were at one time prisoners to the King, but nobly used and attended every one according to their rank and quality, who when they were ransomed made it known to their King how honourably they were attended in England, and what respect the King and our English nation shewed them being prisoners who might have taken their lives away as well as their persons prisoners.

The second thing that was remarkable in Sir Richard Whittington's year was that the King kept his Christmas at Lambeth, and at the feast of Purification seven Dolphins of the sea came up to the River of Thames and played there up and down until four of them were kill'd.

On Saturday the eve of St. Michael the Archangel the year following, in the morning before day, betwixt the hour of one and two of the Clock, began a terrible earthquake with Lightning and thunder which continued the space of six hours, and that universally through the whole world, so that most men thought the world as then would have ended. The unreasonable beasts roared and drew to the town with a hideous noise, also the fowls of the ayr cryed out, such was the work of God at that time to call his people to repentance.

The four and twentieth day of January following a battel or combat was fought in Smithfield within the lists before the King between the men of Feversham in Kent, John Upton Notary Appelant and John Down Gentleman defendant. John Upton accused John Down that he and his compiers should design the King's death on the day of his Coronation following. When they had fought somewhat long and received each of them some wounds, and still persisting in their violent action and no hopes to find out the truth, the King took up the matter and forgave both parties.

On Candlemas eve following in divers places of England was great weathering of wind, hail, snow, rain with thunder and lightning, whereby the church of Baldock in Hertfordshire and the church and part of the town of Walden in Essex, with other neighbouring villages, were sore shaken, and the steeple of St. Pauls in London about two in the afternoon was set on fire in the midst of the shaft first on the west side and then on the south, and divers people espying the fire came to quench it in the steeple, which they did with vinegar, so far as they could find, so that when the Lord Mayor with much people came to Pauls to have holpen if need had been they returned again every man to his own home, trusting in God all had been well, but anon after between eight and nine of the clock the fire burst out again afresh out of the steeple, by reason of the wind more hot and fervent then before, and did much hurt to the lead and timber thereof. Then the Lord Mayor and many people came thither again and with vinegar quenched the fire which was so violent, but no man received any hurt.

Moreover in Sir Richard Whittington's time lived one Richard Fleming, Bishop of Lincoln, in the year 1430 who founded Lincoln Colledge in Oxford, which was afterwards in Richard the third's time in the year of our Lord 1479 by Thomas Rotherham Bishop of the same sea (*sic*) much augmented and enlarged with great revenues. Likewise Magdalen Colledge in Oxford was built by William Wainfleet Bishop of Winchester, who was a loving and constant friend to Sir Richard Whittington and did much good in many parts of this kingdom, and the said Sir Richard did largely contribute to these and the like pious uses by the intreaty of this Bishop.

In the year of our Lord 1419, in which Sir Richard Whittington was the third time inaugurated into the Mayoralty as is before mentioned King Henry the fifth, who having conquered the greatest part of France and espoused Katherine sole daughter to the King and heir to the crown, taking leave of his father-in-law, embarked with his Royal bride and landed at Dover upon Candlemas Day, leaving in France for his deputy his brother the Duke of Clarence, from thence arrived in London the fourteenth day of February, and the Queen came thither the one and twentieth day of the same month, being met upon Black-Heath by the Lord Mayor and three hundred aldermen and prime citizens in gold chains and rich costly habits with other sumptuous and brave devices as pageants, speeches and shows to the great delight and content of both their Maiesties.

The four and twentieth day of February following being St. Mathew's Day her coronation was solemnized in St. Peter's Church in Westminster; which being ended, she was afterwards royally conveyed into the great hall and there under a rich canopy of State sat to dinner, upon whose right hand sate at the end of the table the Lord Archbishop's grace of Canterbury and Henry called the rich Cardinal Bishop of Winchester, upon the left hand of the Queen sat the King of Scots in a chair of State, and was served with covered dishes, as the Bishops were. But after them and upon the same side next to the Boards end were seated the Dutchess of York and Countess of Huntington, the Earl of March holding a scepter in his hand, kneeling upon the right side, the Earl Marshal in the like manner kneeled upon the left hand of the Queen: the Countess of Kent sat under the table at the right foot, and the Countess Marshal at the left foot of her Majesty.

Humphery Duke of Glocester was that day overseer and stood before the Queen bareheaded, Sir Richard Newel was carver and the Earl of Suffolk's brother cup-bearer, Sir John Stewart, Sewer, the Lord Clifford (instead of the Earl of War-wick) Pantler, the Lord Willoby (instead of the Earl of

Arundel) chief Butler, the Lord Gray Caterer, Naperer, the Lord Audley (in the stead of the Earl of Cambridge) Almner, the Earl of Worcester was Lord high Marshal, who rode about the Hall on a great courser, with many tip-staves about him to make room in the Hall. In the which Hall next after the Queen, the Barons of the Cinque Ports began the table, upon the right hand towards St. Steven's Capel (*sic*), and beneath them at the table sat the Vouchers of the Chancery, and upon the left hand next to the cupboard sat Sir Richard Whittington (now the third time Lord Mayor) and his brethren the Aldermen of London. The rest of the Bishops began the table over against the Baron of the Cinque Ports, and the ladies and chief noble-women the table against the Lord Mayor and the Aldermen, at which two tables of the Bishops the Bishop of London and the Bishop of Durham sat highest at the one and the Countess of Stafford and the Countess of March on the other. And for ordering of the service divers chief lords were appointed officers as Steward, Controuler, Surveyor, and the like, which places were supplyed by the Earls of Northumberland and Westmorland, the Lord Fizmur, the Lord Farneval, the Lord Gray of Wilton, the Lord Feres of Groby, the Lord Poynings, the Lord Harrington, the Lord Ducy, the Lord Daker, the Lord Delaware, &c.

I have shewed you onely the ordering of this rich feast, but the cost and sumptuousness of the fare would ask too long and large a circumstance to discourse; what I have hitherto done was onely to show to the world that at those high solemnities inaugurations and coronations the Lord Mayor of the City of London and the Aldermen have place, and their presence is still required; the City being the King's Chamber and in an inter-regnum he the first and prime officer in the kingdom. But I fear I have dwelt too long on the premises which I hope none will hold for an unnecessary deviation. I come now to discourse unto you of Sir Richard Whittington's invitation of the King and Queen into the City when he bountifully feasted them in his own house at his own proper charge.

How great and magnificent the Londoners feasts be even amongst themselves especially at that high and pompous festival at Guild-Hall the day after Simon and Jude, at the solemn inauguration of his Lordship who but knows, as also the ordinary Tables of the Lord Mayor and the Sheriffs where there is free and generous entertainment for all men of fashion and quality, the like both for plenty of dishes and order of service is not elsewhere to be or found through Europe. If then their daily provision be so curious and costly, what may we think their variety and rarity was at the invitation and entertainment of two such great majesties? I must therefore leave it to the Readers imagination being so far transcending my expression. Let it therefore give satisfaction to any one that shall doubt thereof, that it was performed to the everlasting reputation of the honour of the city and great content of these royal personages invited. The bounty of the table not to be question'd.

E

I come now to the fire that he made in the Presence chamber
where the King and Queen then dined, which was only of
sweet and odoriferious (*sic*) wood, far exceeding the smell of
juniper, for it was mixed with mace, cinnamon, and other rare
and costly spices, which did cast such a pleasant and delightful
savor through the room that it pleased his majesty to call him
unto him and say, my good Lord Mayor, though your fare be
choice, costly and abundant, yet above all things I have observed
in your noble entertainment this fire which you have provided
for me gives me more content.   To whom Sir Richard
Whittington making a low obeysance made answer, It much
rejoyceth me dread Soveraign that any that remaineth in my
power can give your highness the least cause to be pleased,
but since you praise this fire already made I purpose ere your
sacred majesty depart the house to entertain you with one (I
hope) that shall content you much better.   The King not
thinking it could be possible desired him to make a proof thereof,
when he (having before provided himself for that purpose)
brought a great bundle of Bonds, Indentures and Covenants
under his arm, said thus to the King, Royal Soveraign to
whom I owe both my fortunes and my life, I have here a faggot
of purpose left for this fire, which I hope will smell much more
sweetly than the first in your nostrils, for saith he, here is
first your Highness security for ten thousand marks, lent you
for the maintainance of your royal wars in France, by the
Right Worshipful Company of the Mercers, which I here

cancel and cast into the fire, fifteen hundred lent by the City to your Majesty I send after the former, two thousand marks borrowed of the Grocers Company, three thousand of the Merchant Taylors, one thousand of the Drapers, one thousand of the Skinners, one thousand of the Ironmongers, one thousand of the Merchant Staplers, of the Goldsmiths three thousand, of the Haberdashers as much, of the Vintners, Brewers and Brown Bakers three thousand marks. All these you see are cancel'd and burnt, saith he, with divers other bonds for money lent by my father in law Aldermen Fitzwarren for the payment of your souldiers in France, which coming unto me by executorship I have taken in and discharged.

Others there likewise due to me of no small sums by divers of your nobility here present, all which with the former I have sacrificed to the love and honour of my dread sovereign, amounting to the sum of three score thousand pounds sterling, and can your Majesty (saith he) desire to sit by a fire of more sweet scent and savour? At this the King was much extasi'd and the rather because it came unexpectedly and from so free a spirit, and embracing him in his arms said unto him that he thought never King had such a subject, and at his departure did him all the grace and honour that could descend from a King to a subject, promising him moreover that he should ever stand in the first rank of those whom he favoured. And so the Lord Mayor bearing the sword before their two most sacred Majesties as far as Temple Bar the King for his former service and his most

F

kind and loving entertainment at that time, and the noble men for that extraordinary courtesie offered them all unitely (*sic*) and unanimously commended his goodness, applauded his bounty and wished that he might live to perpetual memory and so bid both him and the City for that time adieu.

To omit all other circumstances having acquainted you with the poor and mean estate of this Sir Richard Whittington when he came first into the City of London, and by what means he was relieved in his miserable poverty, as also the fortunate success of his small adventure whereby he was raised unto so great honour, that he became the Cities Governour, and how discreetly and wisely he behaved in his authority and office, gaining thereby the love and probation (*sic*) of all men. And further having shewed you what goodly buildings have been raised by his great cost and charge, as one church, two colledges, and certain almshouses, with yearly means left for the maintenance of all such as shall be admitted into them, and many other charitable acts performed by him which are before related, to the great good and benefit of the City, and what things of note happened in his time, I will now conclude with Master Stow, O that London had a Park near adjoining to it, stored with such Deer (as doubtless it hath, though not easily known) for some build Alms houses, free schools, causies and Bridges in needful and necessary places, others repair ruinated and decayed churches, relieving Hospitals in a bountiful manner, and are weekly benefactors to Prisons and those performed by such agents faithfully, that the true bestowers are not publicly noted, howsoever they may be easily supposed. But the glory they seek to invade here will (no doubt) for ever shine on them elsewhere. And that great God who hath created us, and plentifully distributed in his great bounty all things to men, and yet not given all things to any one man, lest it might take away that necessary commerce and mutual society which ought to be amongst us, stir up the minds of more of them to imitate at least, though not to exceed them in their bounty and liberality.

FINIS.

Lightning Source UK Ltd.
Milton Keynes UK
UKHW050603181222
414012UK00026B/126